CHEER
FEARS

BY JAKE MADDOX

text by
Rachel Smoka-Richardson

STONE ARCH BOOKS
a capstone imprint

Published by Stone Arch Books, an imprint of Capstone
1710 Roe Crest Drive, North Mankato, Minnesota 56003
capstonepub.com

Library of Congress Cataloging-in-Publication Data
Names: Maddox, Jake, author. | Smoka-Richardson, Rachel, author.
Title: Cheer fears / Jake Maddox ; text by Rachel Smoka-Richardson.
Description: North Mankato, Minnesota : Stone Arch Books, an imprint of Capstone,
[2022] | Series: Jake Maddox JV mysteries | Audience: Ages 8–11. | Audience: Grades 4–6.
| Summary: Soon-to-be eighth graders and close friends Robert, Maryam, and Kiley are
excited to be at sleepaway cheer camp this summer, even after they find out that their
cabin is supposed to be haunted. Ghost stories are fine, but then the pranks start and
the accusations start flying. Robert is the only one in the whole cabin who has not been
pranked, so he thinks that he better figure out who is responsible before he gets the blame.
Identifiers: LCCN 2021033219 (print) | LCCN 2021033220 (ebook) | ISBN 9781663975140
(hardcover) | ISBN 9781666330144 (paperback) | ISBN 9781666330151 (pdf)
Subjects: LCSH: Cheerleaders—Juvenile fiction. | Camps—Juvenile fiction. | Practical
jokes—Juvenile fiction. | Friendship—Juvenile fiction. | Detective and mystery stories.
| CYAC: Mystery and detective stories. | Cheerleading—Fiction. | Camps—Fiction. |
Practical jokes—Fiction. | Friendship—Fiction. | LCGFT: Detective and mystery fiction.
Classification: LCC PZ7.M25643 Cj 2022 (print) | LCC PZ7.M25643 (ebook) | DDC 813.6
[Fic]—dc23
LC record available at https://lccn.loc.gov/2021033219
LC ebook record available at https://lccn.loc.gov/2021033220

Designer: Heidi Thompson

Image Credits: Getty Images: David Madison, cover

TABLE OF CONTENTS

FIRST CAMP CHEER

"A-W-E!" *Clap-clap.* "S-O-M-E!"

A row of ponytailed girls pumped their fists in the air to the sounds of pulsing music. Two boys turned flips across the mat. The audience clapped and whistled.

And Robert loved it all.

Seventh grade was finally over. It was Monday afternoon, and Robert sat on the bleachers of the North Point Cheer Camp gymnasium. His best friends, Maryam and Kiley, sat on either side of him, squealing with excitement.

Robert's parents had driven the three to camp that morning. After saying goodbye, Robert and the girls grabbed their backpacks and sleeping bags and rushed to the gym for the opening ceremonies.

The cheerleaders posed in their final formation, and the crowd whooped and hollered. Robert had been lifting weights all spring in hopes that he would finally be able to balance Kiley on his hands. She was short and muscular and would make the perfect flyer to his base. As a longtime ballet performer, Maryam preferred the dance moves to the stunts.

A tan woman with shiny blond streaks in her long dark hair walked up to the podium.

"Is this working?" she asked into the microphone.

"YES!" roared the crowd.

"Great," she said. "Welcome to North Point Cheer Camp, the premiere cheer camp in the tristate area!"

More clapping. Someone whistled. Robert

wondered if someone here could teach him to whistle using his fingers.

"First of all," the woman said, "weren't our camp counselors outstanding? Let's give them a huge welcome and thank them for that impressive routine!"

The campers stamped their feet and screamed. *"WOOOOOO!"*

"I am your camp director, Head Coach Jennifer Reyes," she said. "It is my job to make sure that you learn how to be better cheerleaders."

"No kidding," muttered Kiley.

Maryam shushed her.

Kiley was often snarky, and Maryam kept her in line. Robert thought they were like a comedy duo, and he was their happy audience. The three of them made a great team.

Head Coach Jennifer continued. "But becoming better cheerleaders does not only mean perfecting your roundoff back handspring or learning new chants. Cheerleader is made up of two words—

cheer and leader. You are all leaders. You are all representatives of your junior high and high schools. And you need to behave as such."

Robert sighed and wiggled on the bench. He was anxious to get up and do something.

Kiley clearly felt the same way. "If I wanted to be lectured, I would have gone to summer school," she said.

Robert nodded. Maryam reached over and poked Kiley's leg.

Head Coach Jennifer continued. "Also, cheerleading is a team sport. You never see just one cheerleader on the field. There's always a group, and the best ones work together."

She held up a shiny gold trophy. "However, cheerleading is also competitive. You'll be splitting up into small groups and choreographing a short routine. The best teams will win a camp award."

Robert shoulder-bumped his best friends. "We're totally going to win one of those awards," he said.

Maryam nodded, her face framed by her sports hijab. She pulled on the cuffs of her long-sleeved T-shirt under her purple camp T-shirt.

All campers were required to wear camp shirts color-designated by grade. Grade eight had been assigned a dark shade of purple. Robert hated purple, but he didn't complain. He was just happy to finally be at camp.

Head Coach Jennifer motioned with her hand, and a tiny girl with long black hair stood up. Robert recognized her as the top flyer in the final formation. Her giant red bow swished as she walked.

"I'd now like to introduce you to my assistant camp director, Coach Amber Lee," said Coach Jennifer.

Coach Amber bounced up onto the platform and waved her arms.

"Hey there campers, are you ready to cheer?" she shouted.

The crowd stamped their feet on the bleachers.

She cupped her hand to her ear. "I can't hear you . . . I said, are you ready to cheer?"

Screams filled the gym, and Robert felt himself swept up in the crowd as they all stood and waved their arms.

The rest of the counselors swarmed around Coach Amber.

"Repeat after me!" she called. "We've got spirit, yes we do! We've got spirit, how about you?"

The cheerleaders clapped in staccato rhythm, and at the end of the cheer, pointed their poms at all the campers on the bleachers.

The campers responded, "We've got spirit, yes we do! We've got spirit, how about you?"

This went on for several rounds, until the counselors responded with cheers and leaps. A couple of the shorter girls flipped and landed on the two boys' shoulders. Coach Amber slid into the splits. The gym got so loud that Robert plugged his ears.

Head Coach Jennifer leaned into the podium.

"All right, everyone, head back to your rooms and settle in. After dinner, we'll start our first master class," she announced.

The stands clattered as the campers stormed out of the gym to their cabins. Robert, Kiley, and Maryam looked at their schedules. All three of them were staying in Oak Manor. Kiley and Maryam would share a room, while Robert would meet his roommate shortly.

Oak Manor was actually a small house-like cabin with a wraparound porch and bedrooms on the second and third floors. On the first floor was a large open room filled with tumbling mats and old couches.

Kiley and Maryam headed to the third floor to find their room, while Robert found his room on the second floor. A sign on his door said, *Welcome to North Point Cheer Camp, Robert and Josh!*

Robert opened the door and found a set of bunk beds, two dressers, and two desks.

A tall, dark-haired boy was already in the room, unpacking his duffel bag. He was wearing a green camp T-shirt and black athletic shorts.

"Hey," said the boy, "I'm Josh. Grade Nine. Second year at camp. Camp award winner." He nodded at Robert's purple shirt. "Obviously you're a newbie Eight."

"Yeah," said Robert. Normally confident, he suddenly felt awkward and nervous.

"I guess you're Robert, then," said Josh, pointing to the door sign.

"Oh, yeah, um, that's me," Robert answered.

Josh had already claimed the bottom bunk, so Robert climbed up the ladder and unrolled his sleeping bag. Robert had never slept on a top bunk before.

"I'm here with Ellie and Madison," said Josh. "We're the outgoing tri-captains for the South Valley JV basketball cheer squad."

"Great," said Robert.

"What do you cheer for?" asked Josh.

A voice from out in the hallway called out, "Five minutes to first practice. I repeat, five minutes to first practice!"

"Guess it's time to go meet our coach," said Josh. "But remind me to tell you about Heather, the Ghost of Oak Manor."

A ghost?

CHAPTER 2

TEAM NAMES

Before Robert could ask Josh about the supposed ghost, Josh walked away. Robert followed him downstairs to the tumbling room.

The best thing about the tumbling room was the giant windows that covered almost the whole side of one wall. The screens let the wind and birdsongs in while keeping the mosquitos out.

Coach Amber was standing with a clipboard in the center of the room. She was still wearing her sparkly camp cheer uniform and perky oversized hair bow that perfectly matched the red sequins.

"Hi, campers!" she said. "You must be Josh and Robert." They both nodded.

A muscular girl with two long braids walked into the room, followed by a short girl with glasses. Josh ran over to them and gave them fist bumps. Robert assumed that they were Madison and Ellie. Maryam and Kiley were the last to arrive.

Coach Amber made some marks on her clipboard and looked up.

"Great!" she said. "We're all here!"

She sat on one of the couches, and Kiley and Maryam sat next to her. Robert and the rest of the campers sat on the tumbling mats.

"Let's play an icebreaker game," she said. "We'll each say our name and three interesting things about us. I'm Coach Amber. I've been coming to North Point Cheer Camp since I was in seventh grade. This is my second year as a counselor and first year as the assistant camp director. I just finished my sophomore year of college, and I cheered for the varsity football team. Go Bison!"

She motioned her pen toward Kiley. "Why don't you go next?"

Kiley shuffled her feet. "Um, I'm Kiley, I just finished seventh grade, my favorite color is black, and I have a dog named Taco, because I like tacos."

"I love tacos too!" said Coach Amber. "You choose who goes next."

"Um, you," said Kiley. She nodded to the girl on the floor next to her.

"I'm Madison," said the muscular girl with braids. Her green T-shirt perfectly matched her short plaid skort. "I'm starting high school next year. I play lacrosse, and I will try out for—*and make*—the ninth-grade basketball cheerleading squad."

Robert didn't doubt her for a second.

"You go, Josh," Madison said.

Josh shook his dark curls. "I'm Josh, and I'm the

first ninth-grader to make the varsity football cheer squad in Southwestern High history. I like to play video games, and my favorite subject in school is history."

Robert was nervous. Madison and Josh were only one year older than him, and yet they seemed so confident and sure of themselves. He was so worried about measuring up that he barely heard Josh say, "Hey, roommate, you go next."

Robert licked his lips. "I'm Robert. I just finished seventh grade with Kiley and Maryam. I like to watch the true crimes channel on TV, and I want to be a college cheerleader like the ones in the show *U-Cheer*."

"Don't we all," said Madison, under her breath.

"What was that?" asked Coach Amber.

"Nothing," said Madison. The other girl, who Robert assumed was Ellie, rolled her eyes.

"Maryam, your turn," said Robert. He let out a long breath.

"Hi, I'm Maryam. Robert and Kiley are my

best friends. I also take ballet lessons, and I'm a vegetarian."

"You're so tall and graceful. That must make you a terrific ballerina *and* cheerleader!" said Coach Amber.

Maryam beamed, and Coach Amber clapped her hands. "Okay, Ellie, you finish this up."

Ellie looked at Josh and Madison before she started to speak. In a tiny voice she said, "I'm Ellie . . ."

"Louder, Ellie," Coach Amber said with a smile. "Remember, you need to be loud to be a good cheerleader!"

Ellie took a drink of water from her pink water bottle. Her blond bob grazed her chin.

"I'm Ellie," she began again. "I hope to be a basketball cheerleader with Madison next year. I have two baby kittens, and I like to read."

Coach Amber clapped her hands again. Robert wondered if she was always in cheer mode and couldn't stop clapping.

"Thanks, everyone!" said Coach Amber. "Let me tell you how this is going to work. Normally we split up into teams of four for the small group cheerleading. But since we have six people in Oak Manor, we will split up into two teams of three—the Grade Eights and the Grade Nines. Sound good?"

The campers all nodded.

Coach Amber continued, "I want you to come up with your team name. Then create a short cheer that introduces your team name."

Robert raised his hand. "Can our group go outside to work?"

Coach Amber nodded. "That's fine. Just don't go past the porch. I'll come check on you in a few."

Robert, Maryam, and Kiley went to sit on the porch. There were several big wooden rocking chairs, which Robert loved. He and his family lived in a townhouse with the tiniest yard imaginable. He wanted to get the full camping experience and be outside as much as possible.

"So," said Kiley. "What should we name ourselves?"

Maryam giggled. "How about the Great Eights?"

"*Hmmm,*" said Robert. "Not bad. It rhymes. But let's keep brainstorming."

Maryam was the organized one, and she had brought a notebook. She scribbled notes as Robert and Kiley shouted out name ideas.

Finally, she looked up and said, "We've all been dreaming about being cheerleaders . . . how about the Dream Machines?"

Robert nodded. "I like it." Kiley gave Maryam a high five.

They quickly worked out a short routine and headed back inside. Josh, Madison, and Ellie were already there, sitting down.

Coach Amber said, "Why don't we hear from the Grade Eights first?"

The three lined up. "Maryam!" they shouted, as she stepped forward and made a front hurdle jump.

"Robert!" He launched into a spread eagle. "Kiley!" She finished off with a back tuck.

Maryam and Robert moved together as bases for Kiley, the flyer, to perform a thigh stand.

"Dream Machine!" they shouted in unison.

Coach Amber hooted. "I love it! Now let's hear from you, Grade Nines."

Madison said, "We're going to sit on the floor because it's a wrestling cheer."

The three started pounding the mat and clapping, sometimes crossing arms. "We . . . are . . . the . . . Destroyers. We . . . will . . . destroy . . . you."

Coach Amber woo-hooed. "The Dream Machine and the Destroyers. Fantastic names!" she said. "And now I can see what you're capable of and what we need to work on."

She looked at the Dream Machine and said, "We're going to turn that thigh stand into an extension."

To the Destroyers, she said, "Let's get you standing on the mat! But first, let's all head to dinner and our first big group master class. Afterward we'll have a campfire."

Maybe Josh will tell us about the ghost, thought Robert.

CHAPTER 3

GHOST STORY

After a dinner of spaghetti and meatballs and salad that looked and tasted an awful lot like school lunch, the Dream Machine and the Destroyers headed back to the big gym. The camp was holding a master class on different jumps. Robert was pretty good at the tuck and spread eagle jumps, but his toe touch needed some work.

As they walked back to Oak Manor, Robert could hardly believe how dark it could get out in the woods.

He was glad his mom had bought him a headlamp. It was also cold, so Robert and the others went inside the cabin to grab hoodies and joggers.

A small firepit sat not too far from Oak Manor. Coach Amber placed some sticks and a ball of newspaper in the firepit. Then she used a long-nosed lighter to start the fire. Camp staff had left some larger pieces of wood, and she added a couple of those to the fire.

Once Coach Amber got the fire roaring, she passed around marshmallows and long metal skewers. Robert skewered two marshmallows and held them over the fire. He liked to take his time with his marshmallows, turning them often so they turned a crispy brown all the way around.

Madison sat next to him. She stuck her marshmallows directly into the flame, started them on fire, and blew the marshmallow fire out.

"I like the black, burnt part the best," she said.

She ate them straight off the skewer. Meanwhile,

Robert carefully sandwiched his between a chocolate bar and graham crackers to make a s'more.

Kiley piped up. "Josh, Robert told me you said that there's a ghost living in Oak Manor. I don't believe it."

Josh grinned. "Oh, but there is," he said.

Maryam said, "I don't believe in ghosts." She paused. "But tell us about it anyway."

Josh finished off his third s'more and brushed off his hands.

Robert leaned forward. Josh was being dramatic, but he wanted to hear. Just in case he happened to run into the ghost.

"Many years ago, way back in the 1980s, a camper named Heather came to North Point Cheer Camp," said Josh. "She was a world-class gymnast, headed for the Olympics, maybe. Anyway, she could do fifteen back handsprings in a row. It was a sight to see."

"How would you know what it looked like?" asked Madison. "You weren't even born yet."

"Trust me, I know," Josh said.

Maryam giggled.

Josh continued. "So, one dark night, just like tonight, another girl bet Heather fifty dollars that she couldn't do twenty standing backflips in a row without stopping. Heather, being the world-class gymnast that she was, took the bet."

Josh paused a moment. The only sound was the crackling of the fire.

"So, the Oak Manor campers went back in the tumbling room. Everyone stood in a circle around Heather. She put her hands out, bent her legs, and flipped. One. Two. Three. Everyone started to count her flips. Four. Five. Six."

"Are you going to count all the way to twenty?" Madison asked.

Josh ignored the question. "At around fourteen flips, the girl who bet Heather started to get nervous. She didn't have fifty dollars to give Heather. What if Heather did the impossible? Fifteen. Sixteen. Seventeen."

Josh stood up and started circling behind the group. "At eighteen, Heather started to get dizzy," he said. "But she really needed a new set of poms, so she kept going. But at nineteen, Heather didn't make it all the way around."

Suddenly Josh jumped back to his spot and shouted, "CRASH!"

Everyone screamed, then started to laugh nervously.

"Heather had landed flat on her back. She stopped breathing. She was—*dead*," said Josh, drawing out the last word.

Coach Amber piped up. "Josh, this is an old camp legend. You know it's not true."

She paused, then added, "But it is a cautionary tale about not doing anything stupid and to not practice tumbling moves unless there's a coach present."

Josh kept going. "The next year at camp, the Oak Manor campers swore that during the night, they could hear thumps on the floor and a voice counting to nineteen. And weird stuff started to happen. The front door would open by itself. Things like hairbrushes and shoes went missing. Just little pranks, nothing dangerous. The campers in Oak Manor swore that it was Heather haunting the cabin until she could do twenty backflips."

"How do you know all this?" demanded Kiley.

Josh was smug. "My older sister went to North Point Cheer Camp, and one year she stayed in Oak Manor. Once, she woke up in the middle of the night and went to the bathroom. When she was walking back to her bed, she heard a voice that counted to nineteen and then stopped."

Robert shuddered. Josh's sister had heard the ghost!

Coach Amber picked up a bucket of sand. "Fabulous story, Josh. I'll be listening for the sounds of Heather tonight." She poured the sand into the firepit to snuff out the flames. "But unfortunately, it's time for bed."

Everyone groaned.

"We have an early morning tomorrow," she added. "And our first big group practice."

Robert discovered that he really was tired. He brushed his teeth, put on his pajamas, and crawled into the top bunk. As he drifted off to sleep, he heard a faint voice counting to nineteen, but he was ninety-five percent sure it was Josh.

CHAPTER 4

LOCKED IN

BOOM! A crack of thunder rocked Oak Manor. In the top bunk, Robert felt as though the ceiling would cave in on him.

Maybe that's why Josh sleeps in the bottom bunk, he thought.

Robert's alarm buzzed, and he sighed. He hadn't realized that he would have to get up even earlier for camp than he did for school. And the thunderstorm made it feel like the middle of the night.

He climbed down the ladder and quickly got in the shower. He figured that Oak Manor probably didn't have much hot water, so he wanted to get in first. As it turned out, the cabin didn't have *any* hot water. Robert shivered through the fastest shower of his life.

"Dream Machine! Destroyers!" Coach Amber shouted through her megaphone. "You have five minutes! I repeat, you have five minutes to meet in the tumbling room."

Robert tucked his purple camp T-shirt into his shorts and headed down the hallway to meet up with the girls.

Maryam was already warming up on a mat, her long legs stretched out and her toes flexed. Robert sat down next to her. "Kiley still in bed?" he asked.

"Of course," said Maryam. Kiley hated mornings even more than Robert did.

Josh, Ellie, and Madison were on the other end of the room, showing off their backbends and flips.

"Whoa, wait a minute," said Coach Amber. She rushed into the room. "No tumbling without a coach present." She set her clipboard down. "You of all campers should know that, especially after last night's story."

A bolt of lightning flashed across the sky, and the lights suddenly went out. It was completely black in the cabin. Robert couldn't even see his hand in front of his face.

"Stop. Hold on," said Coach Amber.

Robert heard squeaking across the floor, then saw a flash of light.

"*AAAH!*" screamed Maryam.

"What's going on?" shouted a voice. Then there was a loud *crash!*

The lights came on, and the group could see Coach Amber holding her phone flashlight. Kiley was sprawled out on the floor.

Robert jumped up and rushed over to her. "Are you okay?" he asked.

"I'm fine," said Kiley. "I just tripped over the edge of the mat."

"Or did you?" asked Madison.

"Are you sure it wasn't Heather?" added Josh.

Ellie laughed. "Yeah, are you sure?"

"*Wooooooooooo*," said Madison. She pretended to float around the room.

"Okay, that's enough," said Coach Amber.

The Destroyers snickered. Robert rolled his eyes.

"Let's finish warming up, then we'll head to breakfast and morning group practice in the gym," said Coach Amber.

Just as the group was ready to leave, the thunderstorm ended and the sun came out. Maryam excused herself to use the restroom.

Coach Amber said, "We'll wait for you, Maryam."

"But we need to get to the gym early to get the best spots," Madison whined.

"It's okay," said Robert. "Kiley and I will wait for her."

After the Destroyers and Coach Amber left, Robert asked Kiley, "So, what do you think of our cabinmates?"

Kiley shrugged. "They're kind of rude."

Robert nodded. "I totally agree." They laughed.

BANG! BANG! BANG!

"Help!" called Maryam.

Robert and Kiley rushed to the girls' bathroom.

"What's wrong, Maryam?" shouted Robert.

"Are you hurt?" asked Kiley.

"I'm locked in!" cried Maryam. She kept banging on the door.

Robert wiggled the doorknob. "I can't open it from out here!" he said.

Kiley asked, "Can you kick it open?"

"I can't kick it open!" said Maryam. In a small voice she added, "I already tried."

"Do you know what happened?" asked Robert. "Did it jam up when you closed the door?"

"I don't think so," said Maryam. "I just shut the

door and locked it, like usual. After I washed my hands I tried to turn the doorknob, but it wouldn't budge."

Kiley said, "Maybe Heather the ghost locked you in."

Maryam laughed, just a little.

Robert jiggled the knob again. "We're going to have to go get Coach Amber," he said.

"No!" called Maryam. "It's too embarrassing. And I don't want the Destroyers to know."

"Don't be embarrassed. You can't help that you got locked in," said Robert.

"I'm telling you, this is one of Heather's pranks," said Kiley.

"Could be, I guess." Maryam sighed. "And now I'm hungry."

"Me too," said Kiley.

Robert looked at the doorknob again and noticed a keyhole.

"I just remembered," he said. "One time my little

brother got locked in the bathroom, and my mom was able to get him out by using a knife. She stuck the knife in the keyhole and turned it like a key."

"Can't hurt to try," said Kiley.

Robert looked at his watch. "Breakfast is almost over. I'd better run to the mess hall and get a knife before it closes."

"I'll stay with you, Maryam," said Kiley.

"No, go with Robert," said Maryam. "While he's getting the knife, you can get us something to eat."

Robert nodded. "Now that's good thinking," he said.

"Just hurry!" called Maryam.

Robert and Kiley ran up the dirt path to the mess hall. They could see the Destroyers leaving to head up to the gym.

"Let's try not to run into Coach Amber," whispered Robert. Kiley nodded. "Meet back outside."

They separated, and Robert went to the silverware rack and grabbed three knives, just to be safe. He looked around to make sure Coach Amber wasn't behind him and tore out the front door.

Kiley was already outside, her arms full of bagels and oranges. "They wouldn't let me take the scrambled eggs with just my hands," she said.

"Gross," said Robert. "I wouldn't have eaten your hand eggs anyway."

The two raced back to the cabin. Robert went straight to the girls' bathroom, trying to remember exactly how his mom unlocked their bathroom. He stuck the tip of the knife in the key slot of the doorknob and turned it.

"Try opening it now," he said.

Maryam wiggled the knob. "Still locked," she said.

Robert tried it again, and this time he heard a CLICK.

The doorknob turned and Maryam stepped out. She hugged Robert. "I've never been so happy to see you!" she said.

"Same here," he said, hugging her back. "But let's

hurry up and eat something so we're not too late for morning practice."

The three were sitting on Kiley's bed, unpeeling oranges, when they heard a door open.

"Anyone in here?" a voice called.

"It's Coach Amber!" Maryam whispered. "Robert, get under the bed in case she comes in. You're not supposed to be in our room."

Robert crawled under the bed, and the three were silent until they heard the cabin door shut.

It was weird that Maryam got locked in the bathroom.

But there definitely wasn't a ghost in their cabin.

Right?

CHAPTER 5

CLAPS AND STOMPS

"Glad the Dream Machine could make it for lunch," sneered Josh. "We noticed you missed group practice this morning."

Maryam and Kiley set their trays down at the table next to Robert. He was already eating and trying very hard to ignore Josh.

Madison tossed her ponytail. Robert noticed that she had taken out her braids and tied a giant bow around her ponytail, just like Coach Amber.

"Because you weren't there, we got the prime spot in the pyramid," said Madison. "Get used to being off to the side!"

Ellie laughed and flipped her head, even though she had short hair and no ponytail to toss.

Robert finally looked up. "So is that why you played that prank?"

Josh looked puzzled. "What prank?" he asked. "I have no idea what you're talking about."

Kiley piped up. "Locking Maryam in the bathroom and making us miss practice."

"That's the worst prank ever," said Madison. "If we wanted to prank you, we would come up with something much better than that." The Destroyers laughed.

Coach Amber walked up and set her tray next to Robert. "Where were you this morning?"

Maryam gave the Destroyers the stink eye. "Someone locked me in the bathroom. Robert managed to get me out."

Coach Amber ate a bite of her salad. "You know that there's mandatory attendance for all group practice. Being late or absent without a good reason could get you kicked out of camp."

"Isn't being locked in a room with no windows a good excuse for being absent?" asked Robert. He could feel his cheeks starting to get hot.

"*If* that's the reason," said Ellie. She pushed her glasses up on her nose. "Sounds a little fishy, if you ask me."

Josh took a big gulp of milk and burped. "Now you're probably going to blame Heather the ghost," he said. "Maybe she locked the door."

"There are no ghosts," said Coach Amber. "Look, I covered for you today, but I came back to Oak Manor and no one was there. So I don't know where you were or what you were doing. But I'm not going to get in trouble with Head Coach Jennifer just because you didn't show up for mandatory practice. I need this job to pay for school."

Robert was scared. Coach Amber had been really nice to them so far. But now he was worried she was going to kick them all out. He was not going to leave. He saved up all year so he could go to camp. He wasn't about to be sent home on the second day.

What would my parents think? he thought. *And my cheer coach back home?*

They ate the rest of lunch in silence. When Kiley set her fork on the tray, Coach Amber said, "Let's bus our table and head back to Oak Manor for rest period. Afterward, we'll start working on our small group routines."

During rest period Robert tried to take a nap, but his mind kept spinning with thoughts. Who would want to get them in trouble? Obviously, the Destroyers. Robert vowed to keep a close eye on Josh. He didn't trust him.

Robert must have finally fallen asleep, as the next thing he heard was Coach Amber shouting into that terrible megaphone.

"Five minutes to practice. Come to the main room," she called.

Robert's head hurt, but he still rolled out of bed and climbed down the ladder. He was here to become a better cheerleader.

Coach Amber stood in the main room, handing sheets of paper out to everyone. "We're going to work together on a cheer first, before we split up into our two teams."

Josh waved around his arms and made a ghost sound, and Kiley stuck her tongue out at him.

"That is enough," said Coach Amber. "Josh, you, Maryam, and Madison line up here. You're the three tallest, so you'll be in the back. Ellie, Robert, and Kiley, you'll be in the front. But space out so that the three in the back can stand in your windows."

With a little grumbling, everyone got into place.

"Okay," said Coach Amber. "We're going to read the cheer on the paper together. I'll help you with the rhythm."

Hey, all you football fans,

Let me hear you clap your hands!

(Clap, clap, clap-clap-clap)

(Clap, clap, clap-clap-clap)

Now that you've got the beat,

Let me hear you stamp your feet!

(Stomp, stomp, stomp-stomp-stomp)

(Stomp, stomp, stomp-stomp-stomp)

Now that you've got the groove,

Let me see your body move!

(Hey, hey, ah-ah-ah!)

(Hey, hey, ah-ah-ah!)

"Everybody got it?" asked Coach Amber.

The group nodded.

"You can take this cheer back to your schools and make changes as needed," she continued. "Depending on your squad's size and particular skills, you might want to use different moves. But this is how we'll choreograph it today."

Coach Amber showed them the arm and leg motions and how to clap to make the most noise. She encouraged them to make up their own groove movements for the end.

"Now let's see it all together," she called after the group had learned the choreography.

"Hey, all you football fans . . . ," the cheerleaders began as Coach Amber watched closely.

"Kiley, keep those arms straight!" Coach Amber yelled. "Josh, stay on the beat! Maryam, love that grooving! Woo!"

Robert was having so much fun that he almost forgot about earlier.

When they finished, he raised his hand. "I've got an idea!" he said.

Coach Amber smiled. "Let's hear it."

"How about during the claps we switch rows? And then on the stomps we switch back?" Robert asked. "And during the dance we move to the end of the mat for some tumbling?"

Madison looked impressed. "That's not bad," she said, nodding.

"Let's try it!" said Ellie.

The group did the cheer again, moving back and forth, and ending at the corner of the mat. Everyone then did their own moves. Maryam turned several cartwheels and ended with a tuck jump. Kiley and Robert did diving somersaults over each other. Josh performed a walking handstand. Madison turned a back tuck into the splits. And Ellie stepped into a roundoff double back handspring.

Coach Amber clapped. "Nice work! I like it! Let's take a five-minute break and keep working on it."

Madison scowled. "Can't we move on to something else?"

Coach Amber shook her head. "Cheerleading is all about practice. And practice. And more practice. You'll never be perfect, but practice gets you as close as you possibly can be."

CHAPTER 6

STICKY POMS

Wednesday morning big group practice went by smoothly, and Robert was relieved. He had come to camp to become a better cheerleader, not to chase ghosts and get in trouble.

Head Coach Jennifer had chosen him to be one of the tumblers in front of the pyramid. He could hardly wait for his parents to come to the final performance on Friday. They would be excited to watch him turn a back handspring during the cheer.

Even lunch with the Destroyers wasn't half bad. The group talked about the morning's practice and what it was like to cheer back home. Ellie and Madison talked about teaching the small group cheer they learned on Tuesday to the basketball cheerleaders back home.

Robert walked back to Oak Manor with Ellie and Maryam. Actually, Ellie and Maryam cartwheeled back to the cabin, while Robert judged them on who turned the better cartwheel.

The three of them had actually become friends. Robert was glad. Madison and Josh were okay, but they could be mean.

The three were laughing and out of breath when they got to the cabin. Suddenly they heard shrieking coming from the girls' room. They ran in to find Kiley sitting on the floor. Her poms were covered in sticky caramel sauce and gooey hot fudge.

Kiley looked miserable. "How am I going to be part of the big group cheer without my poms?"

Maryam shook her head. "Ugh. Who would have done this?"

"I guess the Ghost of Oak Manor," said Kiley. She held out a piece of paper with typing on it.

Maryam, Robert, and Ellie read the paper silently to themselves: *YOU THINK YOU'RE GOING TO WIN THE CAMP COMPETITION. THINK AGAIN. HEATHER, THE GHOST OF OAK MANOR.*

"Can ghosts type?" asked Ellie.

Robert shook his head. "There are no ghosts," he said. "This is just another prank."

He turned and looked at Ellie. "Are you sure you don't know anything about this?"

Ellie now looked like she was about to cry. "I would never do anything like this," she said.

"No, but your fellow Destroyers would," Robert said. "Notice only the Dream Machine have had pranks played on them. First Maryam was locked in the bathroom, now Kiley's poms. Doesn't that seem suspicious?"

"I'm telling you that we had nothing to do with this," said Ellie. She turned around and walked out of the girls' room, just as Josh and Madison were coming in.

"Gross! What a mess!" said Josh, laughing. "I guess the ghost struck again!"

"Come on, Kiley, let's go to the bathroom. We can try to clean these up," said Maryam.

"Don't get locked in again!" called out Madison.

Robert was sure it was the Destroyers playing these pranks. Maybe they thought it was the only way they'd win the camp competition. Or maybe they were just mean.

Either way, Robert vowed to himself that he was going to catch them in the act next time. He'd prove that there was no ghost and maybe even get them expelled from camp.

A voice came from downstairs. "Five minutes to practice! I repeat, five minutes to small group practice!" called Coach Amber.

Kiley and Maryam were the last to arrive at practice, with Kiley holding two sad, droopy poms.

"I couldn't get the caramel sauce off them," she said. "It's too sticky. I guess I can't cheer. Maybe I should just go home."

Coach Amber put her arm around Kiley. "It's okay," she said. "Hold on."

Coach Amber jumped up and ran to her room, then came back with two of the nicest, fluffiest gold sparkly poms that Robert had ever seen. She handed them to Kiley.

"Here! You can use mine. I always carry a spare pair of poms." She winked. "You never know when you're going to run into a pom emergency, and today proves that!"

Kiley turned them over slowly, then shook them a little. "Thank you. So much," she said. "This is really nice of you, Coach Amber."

"Okay!" Amber clapped. "Let's start practicing our small group routines. No more talk about ghosts or caramel syrup or locked bathrooms. Just cheerleading."

The Dream Machine went to one side of the room and the Destroyers went to the other.

Robert whispered so the Destroyers wouldn't overhear their ideas. "We need to come up with an amazing routine. Now we really need to beat the Destroyers. Nothing can stop us!"

"Hey, that's good!" said Maryam. "Nothing can stop us. Can we turn that into a cheer somehow?"

While Robert and Maryam planned out the cheer, Robert noticed that Kiley was quieter than usual. Normally she was full of ideas and energy and excitement. It's what made her a good cheerleader. But that day she quietly looked at her loaner poms and agreed with all of Robert and Maryam's suggestions.

Robert figured that she was just upset about all of the weird things happening at camp. Or maybe . . . she was scared of ghosts? She didn't really believe there was a ghost, did she?

Before he could help himself, Robert blurted out, "Kiley, do you believe in ghosts?"

Kiley thought for a moment. "I don't *not* believe in ghosts." She shook her head. "I mean, it's hard to believe or not believe in something you can't even see. Maybe there are ghosts, and maybe not."

Maryam looked surprised. "Really? You actually think there might be a Ghost of Oak Manor?"

Kiley shrugged her shoulders. "Why not? Anything is possible."

Robert stood up. "Come on, let's practice. We can talk about ghosts later."

CHAPTER 7

KNOTTED LACES

Thursday morning the Dream Machine headed to breakfast without the Destroyers. Over eggs and bacon, they privately discussed their small group routine.

Kiley and Maryam couldn't agree on what music they should use for Friday's big competition. Maryam wanted to add some dance moves. Kiley just wanted to tumble through the routine.

As much as Robert wanted to win, he was distracted. He noticed the Destroyers walking out of the cafeteria, probably discussing the next prank they would be pulling in Oak Manor.

Robert picked up his tray. "Let's get back," he said.

He didn't want to give the Destroyers much time alone in the cabin. Who knows what they would do next? And it was time for small group practice anyway. Kiley took one long last gulp of orange juice and the three headed out.

While still on the dirt path, they heard shrieking and a few words not suitable for camp.

"Oh!" cried Maryam. The three ran to the door.

The Destroyers sat in the middle of the tumbling mat frantically trying to untangle three pairs of cheerleading shoes. The shoelaces were tied all together in what looked like hundreds of knots.

Josh looked up. "Thanks a lot, Dream Machine," he said. "You really think you can only win if you sabotage us."

Robert was stunned. "Looks like the Ghost of Oak Manor struck again!" he said.

Madison gave him the meanest glare Robert had ever seen.

"Obviously you're the so-called ghost," she hissed. "Notice that you're the only person who hasn't been affected by one of the ghost's pranks."

"Yeah!" added Ellie.

"How are we going to practice today?" said Josh. "There's no way we can get these untangled."

"I guess your practice is off," said Kiley. "Might as well go home."

Without a word, Madison reached for her iced coffee, took the lid off, and dumped it on Kiley's head. The sticky drink dripped all over her hair and down her shirt.

"If that's how it's going to be . . . ," said Robert, and he poured his ice water down Madison's neck. She screamed.

"It's war!" Madison shouted.

The Destroyers flew at the Dream Machine. The shouting was so loud they didn't hear the door open.

TWEEEEET!

"What is going on here!" demanded Head Coach Jennifer, dropping her whistle.

The six campers froze. Robert felt his face grow hot. Coach Amber was standing right next to Head Coach Jennifer, her hands on her hips.

Head Coach Jennifer narrowed her eyes at the group.

"Coach Amber was just telling me that there have been a number of pranks being pulled in Oak Manor," she said. "And now I find you throwing around water and coffee like absolute hooligans!"

Robert looked down. "It was an accident," he said.

"It was an accident that the entire back of Madison's shirt is soaked and you're holding a water cup?" she asked.

Madison piped up. "It was so not an accident!"

Kiley shook her head and stuck her tongue out. "And your pouring coffee on me was?"

"Head Coach Jennifer," said Josh, "you should

know that out of all the pranks, Robert is the only one who hasn't had one played on him. Doesn't that mean he did it?"

"I really don't care who has been playing pranks. If I hear that one more prank takes place in Oak Manor, all six of you will be sent home, and you won't be invited back next year. And this includes you, Coach Amber. You need to get your cabin under control. This camp has a reputation for excellence, and I won't let you ruin it for everyone." Head Coach Jennifer paused. "Do I make myself clear?"

Silence.

"I said, do I make myself clear?" she repeated.

"Yes," said the campers.

Coach Amber nodded. She looked like she was going to cry.

"Fine, then." Head Coach Jennifer looked down at her clipboard. "I need to head over to Pine Hall to observe their practice. You need to figure out how to untie these shoelaces and clean up this room.

Then you had better start practicing. The camp all-star performance takes place in only two days. You need to be ready to impress the judges."

She paused. "Remember the 'leader' in cheerleader stands for leadership."

She turned around and left the cabin. The banging of the screen door sounded extra loud to Robert.

CHAPTER 8

WHO IS THE GHOST?

After Thursday afternoon's big group practice, Robert stayed behind. He wanted to talk to Coach Amber about what was happening in Oak Manor. She had been part of the camp for years. He thought she might know more about the ghost.

As Coach Amber was packing up her tote bag, Robert walked up to her.

"Hey, Coach Amber," he said. "Can I walk to dinner with you?"

Coach Amber turned to the other coaches. "I'll catch up with you later," she said.

She put her hand on Robert's shoulder. "How are you doing?" she asked. "I know it's been a rough week, and I'm sorry that you're not having the best time at camp."

Robert shook his head. "It's okay," he said. He yanked at the bottom of his shirt, which had come untucked during practice. "Do you believe in ghosts? Ones that pull pranks?"

Coach Amber laughed. "No. But the legend of Heather gets passed down every year." She looked at Robert. "You don't really think a ghost has been causing these problems, do you?"

"No," said Robert. "But it would be so much easier if it was. Then people wouldn't blame me for everything."

"Well, who do you think could have pulled the pranks?" she asked.

"That's the thing—I don't know," said Robert.

"Everyone in our cabin has been pranked, except for me. And I'm not guilty!"

He pulled his water bottle out of his backpack. "It would be hard for anyone else to break into our cabin and lock the bathroom or tie up the shoelaces." He paused for a moment. "Wait a minute. *You're* not Heather, the Ghost of Oak Manor, are you?"

Coach Amber gave him a sad smile. "Nope. Trust me, it's not me. I worked very hard to get into my position at camp. I wouldn't throw it away with some knotted-up shoelaces."

Robert looked down. "No, I guess you wouldn't."

"If my college found out that I had been fired from camp, I might get kicked off the varsity football cheer squad," Coach Amber said. "And I can't afford to go to college without my cheer scholarship. Plus, it's my favorite thing to do at school. Eventually I want to coach my own cheer team."

Robert thought that Coach Amber would make a good head cheerleading coach.

"Yeah, if I got kicked out of camp, I might have to leave my team back at school," he said. "And I'm really worried that someone is going to pull a prank at the showcase tomorrow. Someone could get hurt."

"Can you think of anyone in the cabin who would maybe do this?" she asked.

"Not right now," he said, "but I'll think about it tonight."

"Let me know if you think of something," Coach Amber said. "Or if you need my help."

Coach Amber turned and headed toward the mess hall. Robert went back to Oak Manor to drop off his backpack and meet up with the Dream Machine.

As they stood in the long line for the salad bar, Maryam asked, "Robert, are you okay?"

Kiley said, "We obviously don't think that you're the ghost."

Robert nodded as he used tongs to grab a single leaf of lettuce. He hated salad and planned to fill his plate with pepperoni, chicken, and cheese.

He couldn't stop thinking, *Who is the Ghost of Oak Manor? Why can't I figure it out?*

After dinner, the Dream Machine used the tumbling room to work on their small group routine. Maryam and Kiley worked out a compromise: Kiley got to choose the music and Maryam would choreograph some dance moves.

That night, as he was getting ready to fall asleep, Robert went over all of the clues in his head. Suddenly he sat up in bed.

CRACK!

Robert had forgotten that he was in the top bunk, and he hit his forehead on the ceiling. But he didn't feel a thing.

Robert knew who the Ghost of Oak Manor was.

CHAPTER 9

MYSTERY SOLVED

Friday morning Robert woke up extra early. He needed to take care of business before anyone else could find out. He rolled out of bed and quietly crawled down the ladder. At first, he thought it was an adventure to sleep way up high. But now he was looking forward to going home and sleeping in his own bed.

When he walked into the tumbling room, he saw Josh and Kiley whisper-arguing about something.

He walked up just in time to hear Kiley hiss, "It's none of your business!"

"Oh, it *is* my business," said Josh. He turned to Robert. "I think I've caught our 'ghost.'"

"I know you have," said Robert.

Josh looked surprised. "You do? I was just kidding."

Robert would have felt smug if he wasn't so mad.

"Kiley, I can't believe it took me so long to figure it out," he said.

The color drained from Kiley's face. "What do you mean?" she said.

"I remembered that you were at my house the day that my little brother got locked in the bathroom and we had to get him out," said Robert.

"But you knew to open the door with a knife!" she said. "That's why I played that prank. I thought it would be easy for you to get Maryam out."

"Why didn't you just admit it was a prank?" Robert asked.

Kiley looked away.

Robert put his hands on his hips. "How many millions of times have we gone to Tootsie's Ice Cream?" he asked. "And what do you always order?"

"A chocolate and caramel sundae," Kiley said, in a small voice.

"Dude, you're so smart," said Josh. He looked at Robert in awe. "I really thought the ghost was you."

"I pay attention," said Robert.

He took a step toward Kiley. "Also, what camp have you gone to for the past six years?"

Kiley let out a long breath. "Girl Scout camp, okay?" she snapped and turned away.

"And what did you learn at Girl Scout camp?" Robert asked.

There was a long silence. "How to tie knots," Kiley finally admitted.

"You *are* the ghost!" shouted Josh. He pointed his finger in Kiley's face. "I was just giving you a hard time before. I didn't actually know anything.

But Robert Holmes figured it out! Yes!" Josh fist-pumped the air.

Robert was mystified. "But why?" he asked. "Why would you do this to your friends? And to your own poms?"

Kiley started to cry. "Here's the deal. I don't want to be here. I hate cheerleading. I just want to go home."

Robert's eyes widened. "But you're such a good cheerleader!" he said. "Your roundoff back handsprings are the best in the squad."

"Just because I'm good at something doesn't mean I like doing it," she said.

"So why didn't you just ask to go home?" asked Robert. "Why go to all the trouble to plan these pranks?"

"I was afraid that if I asked to go home you and Maryam wouldn't want to be my friends anymore," Kiley said. "I didn't want to go to camp, but you and Maryam talked me into it. You kept saying how much fun it was going to be, and I almost believed you. But

I haven't been having fun. After we heard about the camp ghost, I decided to pull a couple of pranks." She hiccupped.

"I actually thought I would get caught right away and would be sent home. But no one figured out that it was me, so I kept coming up with new ideas." She wiped her eyes. "I'm not gonna lie, tying those knots was fun."

Josh looked impressed. "You certainly did a good job tangling them up. They're still tied together. Even between the three of us, we couldn't figure out how to untie all the knots. We were worried we might have to perform today in flip-flops."

"Bring them here, and I'll fix them for you," she said.

Coach Amber stepped out of her room. "Well, Kiley, it looks like Robert solved the mystery of the Ghost of Oak Manor."

Kiley swallowed. "Coach Amber, I am so sorry for getting you in trouble with Head Coach Jennifer.

I didn't want to hurt anyone or get anyone in trouble. I just wanted to go home."

Coach Amber put her hand on Kiley's shoulder.

"It looks like you're getting your wish," Coach Amber said. "Unfortunately, you can't participate in any more camp activities. I'll have to bring you down to Head Coach Jennifer's office. Since it's Friday, you can stay at camp until your parents come to pick you up. But we're going to have to call them as well."

Kiley nodded and wiped her eyes.

Maryam walked into the tumbling room. "Why is everyone down here so early?" she asked.

Kiley really started to wail. "I hate cheerleading. I'm the ghost!" she said.

Maryam looked confused, but she walked over and gave her a big hug.

Kiley wiped her face on her purple T-shirt. "You and Robert are my best friends, and now you're never going to talk to me again."

Maryam patted her back. "We will always talk to

you. And I feel bad that you thought you couldn't tell us how you felt. And even if you're not a cheerleader, you're still part of the Dream Machine."

Robert realized something.

"How can the Dream Machine participate in the camp performance this afternoon?" he asked. "It's hard to do a cheer with only two people. Plus, our routine is choreographed for three."

Not being able to compete might be the only thing that could make him upset at Kiley.

"Hold on, I have an idea," said Josh.

He went to the girls' room and called for Madison and Ellie. The three of them huddled and whispered. They turned, nodding and looking excited.

Josh turned to Coach Amber. "Do you think the Dream Machine and the Destroyers could merge into one team?"

Coach Amber shrugged. "I don't see why not. When I walk Kiley up to Head Coach Jennifer's office, I'll talk to her. But I'm sure it will be fine."

Josh grinned and looked at the clock. "Let's go to breakfast now, and we can talk it over in the mess hall. Then we can come back and practice all morning."

Coach Amber nodded. "That's a good plan. I'll stay back and help Kiley pack up."

CHAPTER 10

LAST CAMP CHEER

The gymnasium buzzed with excitement. Families and friends of campers sat in the stands, waiting to watch the camp finale performance. Groups of campers stood in the hallway chattering nervously or silently stretching.

Since it was camp, the cheerleaders didn't have actual uniforms. But they were all wearing their camp T-shirts and shorts. The girls had ribbons in their hair and glittery makeup on their faces. Ellie had added a bit of glitter to Robert and Josh's faces too.

Robert was filled with electricity. This was the first time that he had ever performed in such a large crowd and with so many other cheerleaders. He hadn't seen his parents and brother yet, but he was sure they were there.

Kiley was out in the crowd someplace with her mom and stepdad. She had been allowed to stay to watch the performance. But then she was going home and would be grounded for the rest of the summer. Kiley said that she didn't mind. She planned on practicing her oboe most of the time. She was more interested in band than cheerleading.

Robert heard a *tap-tap-tap* on the microphone.

"Can you hear me?" asked Head Coach Jennifer.

The crowd roared, "Yes!"

She continued, "Welcome, everyone, to North Point Cheer Camp! I'm Jennifer, the camp director and head coach. On behalf of all the campers, we thank you for coming to watch our final performance!"

Robert felt a poke on his shoulder.

"Hey," said Josh, "are you ready?"

Robert grinned. "Totally. And thanks for letting Maryam and me join your group."

The Oak Manor campers (minus Kiley) spent all morning planning a new routine for the small group competition. Robert had to admit that it was better than the routine that the Dream Machine had put together.

"No prob," said Josh. He left for a last-minute drink of water.

Head Coach Jennifer was still talking. "Here's how the performance will go: First off is a megacheer by everyone, then performances from each of the cabins, and finishing up with a cheer from the coaches. We'll then announce the winners of the competition, and you will be free to head home. Now are you ready for some cheers?"

The crowd screamed.

"I present to you, the North Point Cheer Camp Cheerleaders!"

Music blared from the speaker system. All of
the cheerleaders rushed from the hallway into the
gymnasium, jumping and clapping and encouraging
the audience to stand up and clap along. Then all the
cheerleaders got into place, they stood still, and the
music stopped.

Another song came on, and the cheerleaders
pumped their arms.

Robert could see his parents and brother sitting
with Maryam's mom and two sisters. He could also
see Kiley sitting close to the exit with her parents.
She was waving at Robert and Maryam.

Robert smiled at her and winked. Then he and
several girls performed their back handsprings. Coach
Amber had really helped him improve during camp.

The big group routine finished up, and the small
group routines started. The Oak Manor squad was
number six in the lineup, so they quickly put on the
costumes they had created that morning. The camp
custodian had given them some old towels, and Ellie

had transformed them into short ghost costumes with their faces poking out.

Madison said, "Are you ready?" They each put a hand into the circle, the girls holding their poms.

"Oak Manor! Oak Manor! Oak Manor!" they whisper-shouted and stood by the door.

The microphone screeched, and Head Coach Jennifer said, "Next up are the Ghosts of Oak Manor!"

A short pause, and the Ghosts of Oak Manor floated in to the sounds of the *Ghostbusters* theme song. The crowd clapped and whooped.

"*Wooooooo*," they shouted.

The five cheerleaders wove in and out until they got to the center of the mat. They pulled the ghost costumes up and over their heads and tossed them aside, along with the poms.

Josh, Maryam, and Madison lined up in the back, while Robert and Ellie stood in the front. They started to clap and chant a version of the cheer that Coach Amber had taught them.

Hey, all you North Point fans,

Let me hear you clap your hands!

Now that you've got the beat,

Let me hear you stamp your feet!

Now that you've got the groove,

Let me see your ghostly move!

Woooooooooo!

Woooooooooo!

The tumbling started, one person after another. Ellie ended the tumbling moves with an impressive roundoff triple back handspring run. Then it was time for the big finale!

Josh and Maryam, the bases, pushed Madison into an extension. Robert leaned over and boosted Ellie into a shoulder stand. Madison and Ellie grasped hands and pumped their arms in a V to complete the pyramid!

The crowd exploded in applause, but no one clapped harder than Kiley.

Robert released Ellie and then ran over to help the other bases catch Madison as she executed a straight ride basket toss. The girls grabbed their poms and executed a tuck jump followed by a toe touch. Robert gave a loud whistle like Josh had taught him. Josh scooped up the costumes, and they all ran off the mat.

As soon as they were in the hallway, Madison pulled them into a group hug.

"That was so good!" she cried.

They sat down against the wall, panting and sweating, to wait for the results.

Finally, they heard Head Coach Jennifer shout, "North Point Cheer Camp Cheerleaders, it's time to announce this year's winners!"

All the campers ran out onto the mat. There was lots of squealing as Head Coach Jennifer announced several of the small group names.

Finally she said, "I'd like to give this next award to a team that showed grit, cooperation, and creativity—the Ghosts of Oak Manor!"

The five ran up to the podium. Head Coach Jennifer handed them each a small trophy topped with a gold cup. Each trophy was engraved with the words *NORTH POINT CHEER CAMP CHAMPION*.

The event ended, and Robert's family rushed to him and his friends—both old and new—for hugs and photos. The Ghosts of Oak Manor each swapped phone numbers and promised to text as soon as they got home. Coach Amber came over for a group selfie.

Robert said, "I promise to come see you cheer at a football game this fall."

Coach Amber leaned over. "I'm so proud of you for solving the mystery!" She handed him a piece of paper with her school email written on it. "You send me a message to let me know the date, and when you come to that game, I'll get you down on the field for some cheers."

Robert hugged her one more time. "You enjoy the rest of your summer!" she said.

As they walked out to their car, Robert's dad said,

"It looks like you had a great week at camp, Robert! Do you want to come back next year?"

"For sure!" said Robert, as he thought, *I still need to find Heather, the REAL Ghost of Oak Manor!*

photo credit: Caroline Yang

Rachel Smoka-Richardson is the author of several children's books, including *Millicent Simmonds: Actor and Activist* in the Movers, Shakers, and History Makers series. She has an MFA in writing for children and young adults from the Vermont College of Fine Arts. In her free time, Rachel loves to read, craft, travel, and hang out with her husband and sweet rescue dogs at their Minnesota home.

GLOSSARY

choreograph (KAWR-ee-uh-graf)—to plan the movements and words for a cheer or dance

competitive (KUHM-pet-i-tiv)—having a strong need or want to win

hooligans (HOO-li-guhnz)—a group of people who misbehave

manor (MAN-er)—a house on a large area of land

mystified (MIS-tuh-fied)—confused

rhythm (RITH-um)—a regular beat

staccato (stuh-KAH-toh)—short, sharp sounds

tenacity (tuh-NAS-i-tee)—having determination, bravery

tumbling (TUHM-bling)—gymnastic moves on a mat or the ground

DISCUSSION QUESTIONS

1. Kiley was afraid that if she quit cheerleading, her friends would not like her anymore. Have you ever felt that way? How might you have handled Kiley's situation?

2. What clues did Robert use to discover that Kiley had been playing the pranks? Have you ever solved a mystery? How did you solve it?

3. Discuss the pranks Kiley played on her camp friends. Did any of the pranks cross the line into truly harmful territory? Explain your answer.

WRITING PROMPTS

1. Make a list of skills needed to be a good cheerleader. Considering your list, which character in the book was the best overall cheerleader? Write a paragraph explaining your choice.

2. Robert and his teammates worked together to create their final cheer. Write about a time you worked with a team to achieve a goal. Compare your experience to Robert's.

3. Cheerleaders use chants to help get audiences excited about a game or event. Write a cheer that you could perform for a group.

SPOTLIGHT ON CHEER MOVES

There are many tumbling moves used during cheers. Here are some of the moves the Ghosts of Oak Manor used during their routines:

BACK TUCK: In this move, the cheerleader flips backward, bending the knees and pulling the legs into the body while rotating.

TUCK JUMP: In this jump, the cheerleader pulls the legs up with the thighs as close to the chest as possible. The knees face upward in a tucked position.

SPREAD EAGLE JUMP: In this jump, the cheerleader's arms are in a high V and the legs are spread to create an X shape with the body.

ROUNDOFF: This move is similar to a cartwheel, but both feet land at the same time.

TOE TOUCH: In this jump, the cheerleader's legs are spread apart, pointing straight out to the sides and parallel to the ground, toes pointed. The arms are also spread out to touch the fingers to the toes.

BACK HANDSPRING: In this move, the cheerleader does a complete revolution by lunging backward headfirst with the arms outstretched. The hands touch the ground and then immediately push off, springing back to an upright position.

THIGH STAND: This stunt involves three cheerleaders, plus a possible spotter. Two cheerleaders form the base by side lunging toward each other. The flyer then steps onto the bases' thighs. The bases each wrap an arm around the flyer's knees, and the flyer's arms are lifted to form a V.

SHOULDER STAND: In this stunt, a flyer stands on a base's shoulders.

STRAIGHT RIDE BASKET TOSS: In this stunt, the bases throw a flyer into the air. The flyer's arms are fully extended next to the ears and the body is in a straight position. Keeping the extended position, the flyer then lands back into the bases' arms.

SOLVE ALL THE SPORTS MYSTERIES!

JAKE MADDOX JV MYSTERIES

CHEER FEARS

JAKE MADDOX JV MYSTERIES

OFF BASE

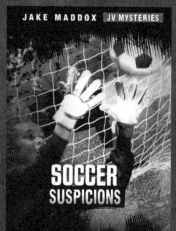

JAKE MADDOX JV MYSTERIES

SOCCER SUSPICIONS

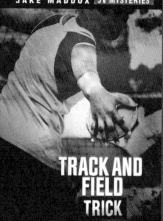

JAKE MADDOX JV MYSTERIES

TRACK AND FIELD TRICK